Sandy Creek
NEW YORK

An Imprint of Sterling Publishing
387 Park Avenue South
New York, NY 10016

Copyright © 2013 by Parragon Books Ltd
Text © Hollins University

This 2013 edition published by Sandy Creek.

Written by Margaret Wise Brown
Illustrated by Charlotte Cooke

ISBN 978-1-4351-4926-7

Manufactured in Heshan, China
Lot #:
2 4 6 8 10 9 7 5 3 1

07/13

SUNSHINE
and
Snowballs

Sandy Creek
NEW YORK

Summer, summer in the sun,

Flowers grow and bunnies run.

Snowballs, snowballs in the snow,

Snowflakes fall and cold winds blow.

Pussy willows in the spring,

Violets bloom and birds sing.

The wind blows hard across the hills,

And shakes the yellow daffodils.

Grasshoppers,
ladybugs,
and bees,

Hop about, bare toes and knees.

The fog comes on without a sound,

Gray, silent, all around.

Rain, rain on the windowpane,

Splashes once,

then splashes again.

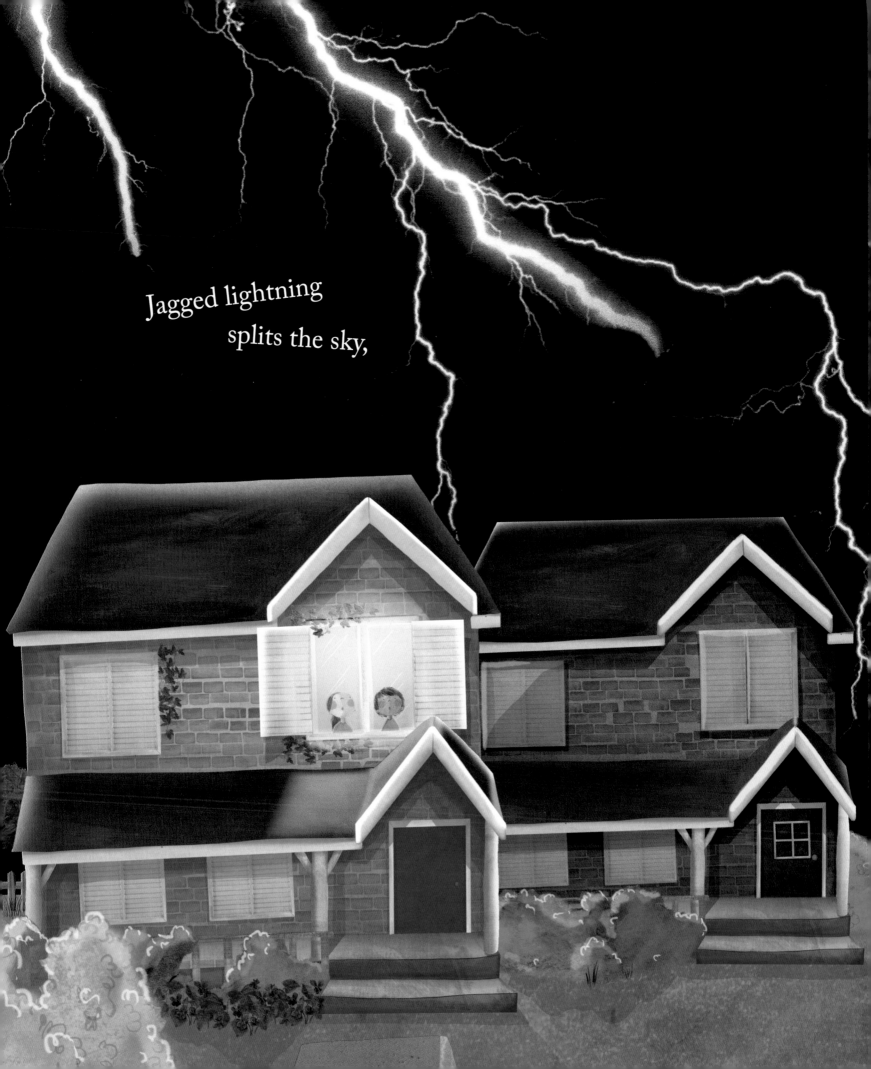

Jagged lightning
splits the sky,

Thunder rumbles, wild winds cry!

Orange pumpkins, yellow corn,

Purple grapes and a frosty morn.

Smoke is drifting all around,

From raked leaves
on the ground.

Walk across the icy snow,

Footprints follow wherever you go.

Starlight, starlight, frosty bright,

Fills the spaces of the night.